WHERE'S WALLY?
TAKES FLIGHT
MARTIN HANDFORD

WALKER BOOKS
AND SUBSIDIARIES
LONDON • BOSTON • SYDNEY • AUCKLAND

WIZARD
WHITEBEARD

WALLY

ODLAW

WENDA

WOOF

HI, FANS!

LET'S SOAR UP INTO THE
SKIES ON AN AVIATION ADVENTURE
PACKED FULL OF LOOP-THE-LOOP CHAOS!

POWER UP YOUR BRAIN-ENGINES TO PLAY
PUZZLING PUZZLES ALONG THE WAY! ALSO
HELP ME FIND A PHENOMENAL FEATHER!

AND THAT'S NOT ALL! WHEREVER WE GO, WOOF, WENDA,
WIZARD WHITEBEARD AND ODLAW GO TOO. CAN YOU
SPOT OUR LOST THINGS FROM UP IN THE AIR?

WALLY'S   WOOF'S   WENDA'S   WIZARD   ODLAW'S
KEY   BONE   CAMERA   WHITEBEARD'S   BINOCULARS
                                     SCROLL

ENJOY THE BIRD'S-EYE VIEW, HIGH-FLYERS!

Wally

DESTINATION EVERYWHERE

Unscramble the letters in the "Destination" column to spell the names of twelve cities. Then search for flights with "WAL" in them to find out which places I'll be travelling to. Wow!

Depart	Destination	Flight	Arrive	Delays
10:00	WEN OYKR	WAL1	22:00	ON TIME
08:00	NOONLD	WDA1	07:00	ON TIME
22:00	GNHO NKGO	WOF1	10:30	1 HOUR
11:30	RASIP	WOF2	21:00	ON TIME
23:00	BUDAI	ODW2	06:00	ON TIME
22:00	AOS AULOP	WAL2	10:00	ON TIME
13:00	STERAMDAM	WZD1	21:00	1 HOUR
21:00	OTONTOR	WZD2	23:00	ON TIME
23:00	KYOTO	WAL4	13:00	ON TIME
10:00	REOM	WAL3	23:00	ON TIME
19:00	SOLO	ODW1	22:00	3 HOURS
07:00	DNEYYS	WDA2	09:00	ON TIME

MORE THINGS TO DO

★ Did Wally catch all four flights? Starting with "WAL1", check the arrival time matches the departure time of "WAL2" and so on. Can you also find Wenda, Woof, Wizard Whitebeard and Odlaw's abbreviated names? Can you work out where they flew to and if they caught their flights too?

UP IN THE CLOUDS

Ta-da! Help Wizard Whitebeard hop to the finish by moving in repeated sequences of yellow, pink, white and then blue clouds. You can only hop to a cloud that is close by!

START

FINISH

HOT-AIR RACE

Clowns don't like to follow rules! Work out which
hot-air balloon is winning and which ones are disqualified.
You'll go oogly-boogly-woogly-eyed!

To enter the race:

- A hot-air balloon must be manned by three clowns and no one else.

- One clown must wear a bow tie;

- a second clown must wear a top hat;

- and a third clown must wear a red nose.

- Stripes or spots cannot be worn by the same clown.

- No custard pies allowed!

- A hot-air balloon basket must be bobble hat shaped.

SUPER SWARM

Find five floating balloons with real pictures of me and my friends on them (for Woof, all you can see is his tail – it has five red stripes!).

MORE THINGS TO FIND

- A wand
- Two pilots in paper aeroplanes
- A three-tiered cake
- A toy dinosaur
- A hot-air balloon
- A toy arrow
- Four flying rockets
- A crashed toy spaceship
- A yellow flag

BIRD SEARCH WORDSEARCH

Find the name of each furry flying friend in this frame of letters – the words go forwards, backwards and diagonally. Squawk!

- Eagle
- Wren • Gull
- Vulture • Emu
- Crow • Cuckoo
- Mockingbird
- Woodpecker
- Wagtail

MORE THINGS TO FIND

- The word "Odlaw"
- An upside down bobble hat
- A dinosaur
- A very long snake
- Five monkeys
- Four bats
- Two witches
- Sixty-six yellow-and-black striped birds

BIRDS OF A FEATHER

Match each flying creature, machine, person or thing in the sky to another one (or more) of the exact same to reveal an odd one out.

MORE THINGS TO DO

❋ Feathers are ticklish, are you? Tell this joke to a friend and see if it makes them laugh out loud: Why does a seagull fly over the sea? If it flew over Dragon Town it'd be called a dragontowngull!

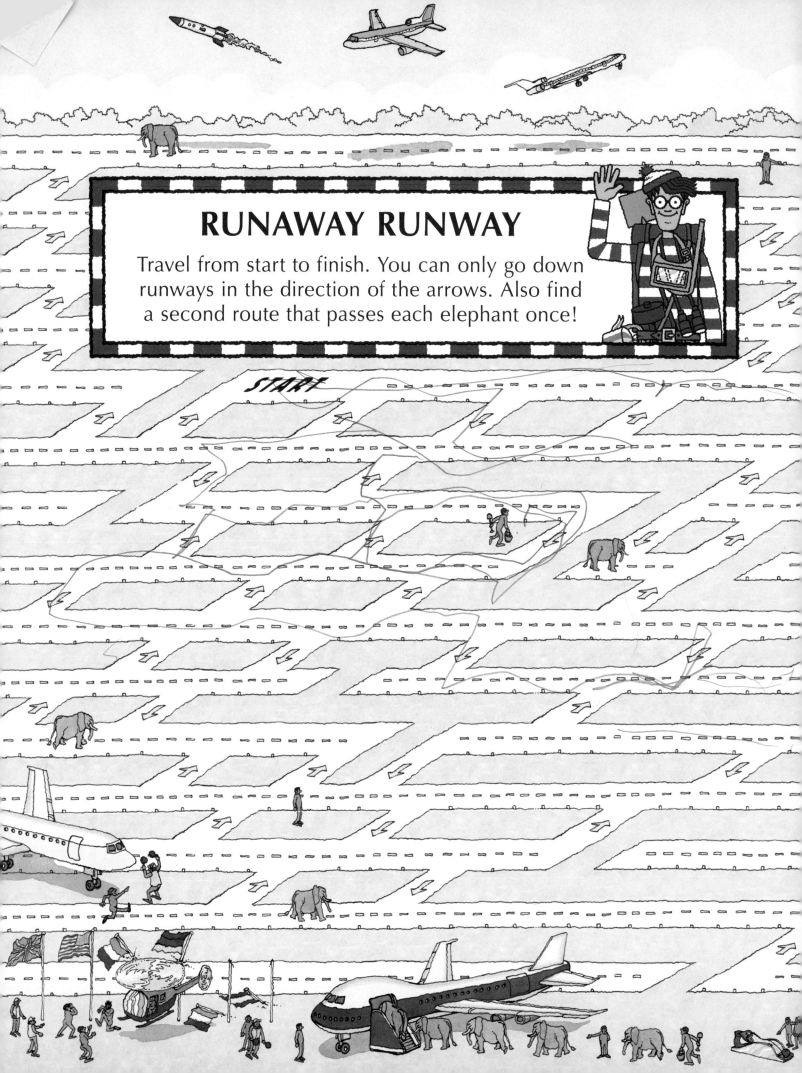

RUNAWAY RUNWAY

Travel from start to finish. You can only go down runways in the direction of the arrows. Also find a second route that passes each elephant once!

START

FINISH

MORE THINGS TO FIND

- [ ] A rocket
- [ ] A wind-sock
- [ ] A flying ace
- [ ] An open suitcase
- [ ] A French flag
- [ ] Three buckets

13

DRAGON MEDAL MAYHEM

What a day of exciting races! Can you match each dragon to the medal that it won? Read all seven descriptions closely and study the pictures on the medals for clues.

HANSEL DUSTY

A greedy dragon who likes anything shiny. A good sense of smell (but very bad breath!).

Sense of direction: high

Sneakiness: high

Strength: big claws for grabbing

THE FORTY WINKS RACE

SUNNY-SIDE-UP SID

A happy-go-lucky dragon who likes to see things from a different perspective.

Sneakiness: low

Sense of direction: low

Intelligence: not so smart!

THE NUMBER CRUNCHING RACE

52
49

EDWINA SHARP

A dreadfully competitive dragon with a bad temper and an extra pointy arrow tail.

Top speed: very fast

Battle power: high

Strength: long claws to sharpen swords

THE NAVIGATION RACE

CORNELIUS COMPASS

A witty dragon who has a sleek coat of scales for aerodynamic tailwind.

Top speed: very fast

Sense of direction: exceptional, can read maps

Intelligence: high, likes to crack wise jokes!

THE UPSIDE DOWN RACE

COUNT BILL CRUNCH

A dragon who is always hungry … for maths sums!

Sneakiness: high

Strength: sharp fangs

Intelligence: high, can use his scales to count in multiples of nine

THE SWORD FIGHTING RACE

BUMP-IN-THE-NIGHT BERNIE

A scary dragon who can float without flapping its wings. Likes to shout "Boo!".

Sneakiness: exceptional, is a ghost

Intelligence: medium, can see through people

Magic: will grant wishes, if you can catch her

THE TREASURE HUNT RACE

SNOOZY VAN WINKLE

A toothless dragon who prefers night-time to day. Can sleep for a year at a time.

Sense of direction: low

Tickle tolerance: low, giggles at the sight of feathers

Strength: squidgy raised scales to soften the blow of bumping into things

THE NIGHT FRIGHT RACE

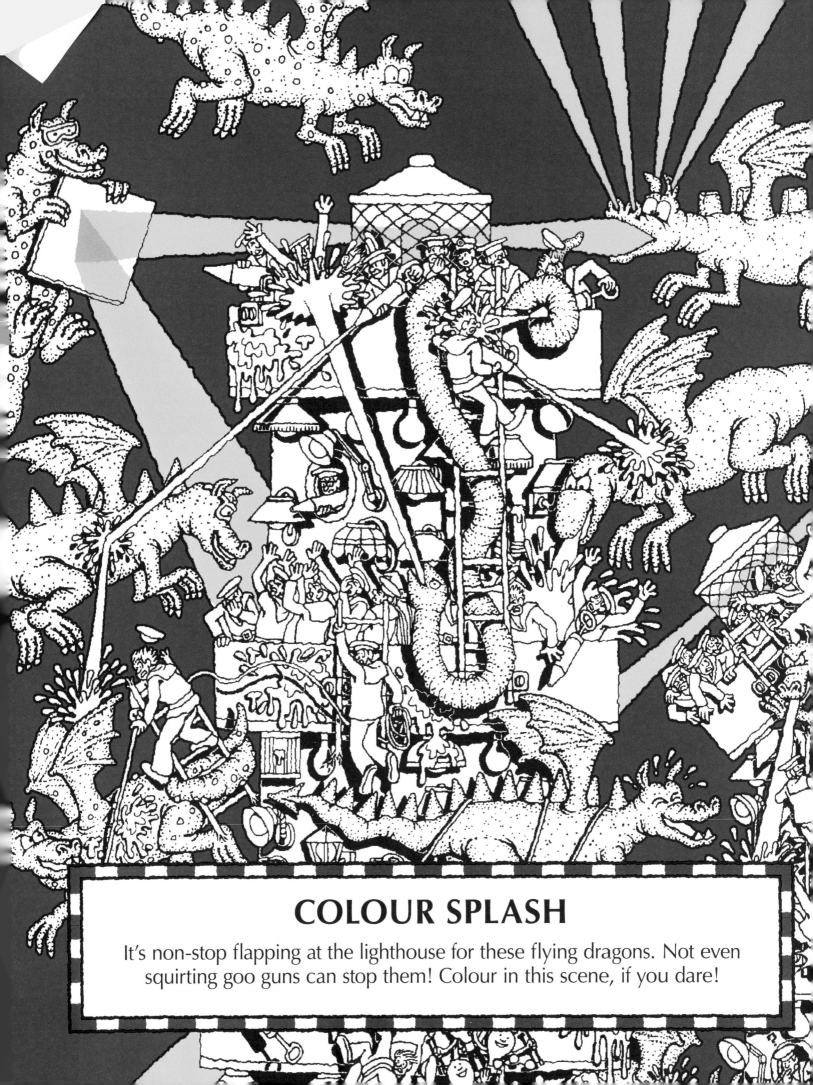

COLOUR SPLASH

It's non-stop flapping at the lighthouse for these flying dragons. Not even squirting goo guns can stop them! Colour in this scene, if you dare!

BALLOON BINGO

Circle a number in the grid if you also see it on one of the ship balloons. Can you get five in a row?

1	7	18	6	12
25	19	2	15	21
10	3	17	22	5
14	8	11	23	16
9	20	24	13	4

MORE THINGS TO DO

✴ How did you win? Was it a line of vertical, horizontal or diagonal numbers? Keep searching if you didn't get all three lines!

TAKE-OFF TEN

What wacky airborne entertainment! Can you spot ten differences between each pair of scenes?

LUGGAGE LOOP

There's lots of chaos going on around this airport conveyor belt! Can you find your way through the luggage tags, lost luggage and crowds of people to the finish?

Read the instructions before you set off.

- **Begin at the start and go forwards either one or three squares.**

- **Move the number of squares as shown – but remember, a yellow luggage tag takes you forwards and a red one backwards. When you land on both at the same time, you choose the direction.**

- **If you land on a square with a single suitcase or bag, move to another identical image and then move forwards five.**

- **If you land on a picture square, search for it in the scene and then move forwards five.**

FINISH

PLANE SNAP

Can you pair up eight sets of two plane
playing cards? Study each one very closely.
Chocks away!

WELL DONE, WALLY-WATCHERS! DID YOU CATCH SIGHT OF THE FEATHER? IF NOT, THERE'S STILL TIME TO SEARCH FOR IT AGAIN!

WAIT, THERE'S MORE! LOOK BACK THROUGH THE PICTURES TO FIND THE ITEMS ON THE CHECKLIST AND SHOWN IN THE STRIPY SHAPES BELOW.

FULL THROTTLE AHEAD!

Wally

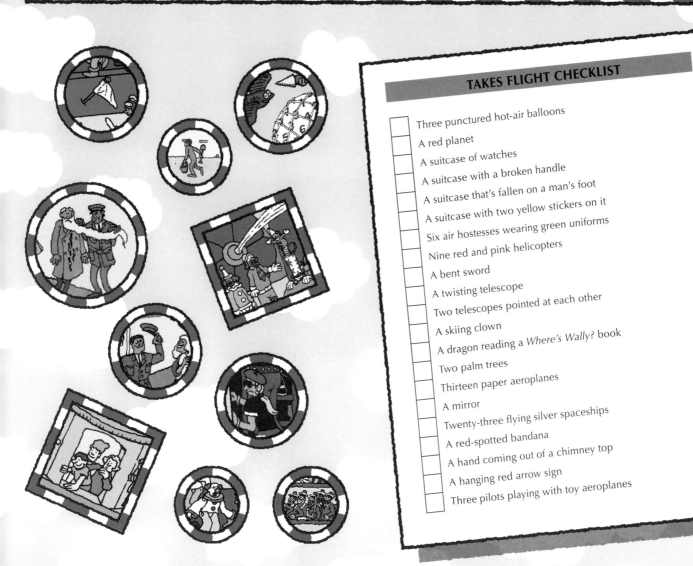

TAKES FLIGHT CHECKLIST

- [ ] Three punctured hot-air balloons
- [ ] A red planet
- [ ] A suitcase of watches
- [ ] A suitcase with a broken handle
- [ ] A suitcase that's fallen on a man's foot
- [ ] A suitcase with two yellow stickers on it
- [ ] Six air hostesses wearing green uniforms
- [ ] Nine red and pink helicopters
- [ ] A bent sword
- [ ] A twisting telescope
- [ ] Two telescopes pointed at each other
- [ ] A skiing clown
- [ ] A dragon reading a *Where's Wally?* book
- [ ] Two palm trees
- [ ] Thirteen paper aeroplanes
- [ ] A mirror
- [ ] Twenty-three flying silver spaceships
- [ ] A red-spotted bandana
- [ ] A hand coming out of a chimney top
- [ ] A hanging red arrow sign
- [ ] Three pilots playing with toy aeroplanes

HERE ARE SOME ANSWERS TO THE HARDEST PUZZLES. DON'T GIVE UP ON THE OTHERS – WHY NOT ASK YOUR FRIENDS TO HELP?

DESTINATION EVERYWHERE

Wally went from New York to Sao Paulo to Rome to Toyko; Wenda went from London to Sydney; Woof went from Hong Kong to Paris; Wizard Whitebeard went from Amsterdam but missed his flight at Toronto; Odlaw went from Oslo but missed his flight at Dubai

UP IN THE CLOUDS

HOT-AIR RACE

BIRD SEARCH WORDSEARCH

RUNAWAY RUNWAY

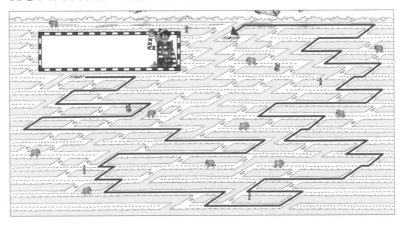

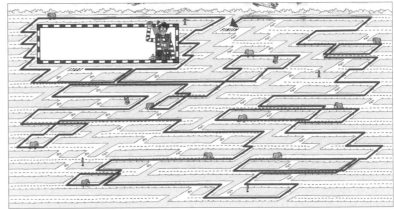

BALLOON BINGO

1	7	18	6	12
25	19	2	15	21
10	3	17	22	5
14	8	11	23	16
9	20	24	13	4

First published 2016 by Walker Books Ltd, 87 Vauxhall Walk, London SE11 5HJ • 2 4 6 8 10 9 7 5 3 1 • © 1987–2016 Martin Handford • The right of Martin Handford to be identified as author/illustrator of this work has been asserted by him in accordance with the Copyright, Designs and Patents Act 1988. • This book has been typeset in Wallyfont and Optima • Printed in China • All rights reserved. • British Library Cataloguing in Publication Data: a catalogue record for this book is available from the British Library. • ISBN 978-1-4063-7060-7
• www.walker.co.uk

ONE LAST THING...

Did you spot a balloon with a clown face on it? If not, then keep on looking until you do! The clown has a bright red nose! Honk, honk!